IF YOU THINK

READING

THAT COULD POSSIBLY BE THE CASE….

(AND A FINE CHOICE OF READING MATERIAL YOU'VE CHOSEN TOO.)

BUT IF YOU HAVE A BLACK SHARPIE AND A WIDE ROLL OF CELLOTAPE IN YOUR POCKET, A HAMMER CLIPPED TO YOUR BELT, A ZOMBIE BIBLE IN YOUR BACK POCKET, AND A CELLOTAPED BAND ROUND YOUR HEAD WITH A MESSAGE ON IT SAYING; *"Don't panic. You're a Zombie. Look in your back pocket. There's a book. OPEN IT AT PAGE ONE"….*

THEN… this is part of a ZOMBIE MEMORY TEST, and you should go directly to PART TWO (2), ZOMBIE STEP 8.

TRUST ME, DON'T ASK ANY MORE STUPID QUESTIONS, JUST GO DIRECTLY TO PART TWO (2), ZOMBIE STEP 8.

YES, PART TWO (2).

ZOMBIE STEP 8….. E.i.g.h.t.

(Zombies; If you're having difficulty doing numbers, just read on……. Whatever.)

The Zombie Bible:

A Zombie Guide to Surviving the Holocaust

(Living as a zombie, and surviving to the end when a vaccine is delivered)

By Ian Hall & Lorraine James

HALLANISH PUBLISHING

This book is a work of fiction. Names, places, characters and incidents are products of the author's imagination or are used fictitiously. Any resemblance to actual events or locales or persons, living, dead or un-dead, is purely coincidental.

Ian and Lorraine are members of Hallanish Publishing.

ISBN-13; 978-1479111176
ISBN-10; 1479111171

The Zombie Bible:

A Zombie Guide to Surviving the Holocaust

(Living as a zombie, and surviving to the end when a vaccine is delivered)

By Ian Hall & Lorraine James

A guide to Zombie statistics;

2 types of statistics will be quoted in this survival guide.

##Zombie Bible WIKI Stat##.... These are statistics drawn from premier sources, which we only use to illustrate points in our thesis. They are proven beyond doubt, and verifiable in most forms of modern media.

##Zombie Bible HAZE Stat##.... The Zombie Bible has surveyed every media source of zombie lore from the early 1960's to the present day, and compiled an average list of statistics based on each film, book, television, and internet source. We endearingly call this list; the "Hollywood Average Zombie Encyclopedia", hence 'HAZE'. We have dumbed down these figures to the nearest one percent.

We realize that you are probably a zombie, and cannot comprehend much more detail than this.

Don't worry your pretty head.

Human Foreword

This book is intended to help you survive the zombie holocaust/apocalypse as a zombie.

Yes, you heard correctly.

##Zombie Bible HAZE Stat## The chances of you contracting the initial zombie virus are 75%. Because of secondary viruses, natural selection, accidents and zombie contact, HAZE reckons that you then have only a 1% chance of surviving as a human through the first 8 weeks. One chance in one hundred.

This means at the average wedding, everyone but you is dead.

Statistics are sometimes very hard facts to read and accept.

This is something you must be prepared for. After 8 weeks, 99% of the general population will one day be like you; zombies.

This new world is a dangerous place, full of sharp edged objects, shambling confused zombies, and panicking, gun-toting humans.

As a human (and therefore able to reason) we assume you have a plan for such an eventuality. If you have not; you better start taking notes. And pretty freaking quickly.

You have to have a plan. And you have to think it through.

But regardless of the complexity of your plan, there are events that you cannot plan for.

"A military plan is only good until the moment of first action."

(Somebody really important, long ago)

##Zombie Bible WIKI Stat## There are 200 million guns in the USA alone, and 117 million households have one. This means that every second house in the country will have one gun.

Now, we all know that zombies don't use guns, so let's do the math, just for the USA.

It's by far the most popular destination of the zombie apocalypse in movies and TV, (probably because of all the failed mortgage banks, inane infomercials, and vapid TV reality personalities), that I feel justified in my choice of statistical location.

USA original population; 300 million.

USA (1%) human survivor population; 3 million.

USA guns; 200 million.

That's 66 guns for every human survivor. That would even make Rambo look like a complete pussy! Now, admittedly, some of those 300 million are too young to use a gun properly, and should be classed as slow moving zombie food, so the figure will recede slightly. But the figure above does not include the 1 million non-USA documented workers, or the 30 million undocumented illegal aliens in the USA, or the 1 million tourists who can be vacationing in the USA or passing through at any time.

There are old people too but, trust me, many older citizens have already exercised their Second Amendment rights, and tooled up with Messer's Winchester and Colt to introduce a quick lesson in lead poisoning to any zombie trespassers. You zombies have to be very careful out there.

And all the movies portray the human survivors as the victims!

So, humans, follow this guide, follow the be-prepared instructions and you'll survive to the end when the helicopters arrive, the human scientists catch you in a net, and pump a vaccine into your poor twitching zombie body.

To survive, you need only follow the rules in this book BEFORE the apocalypse.

You have to prepare for life as a zombie.

Start right now. There's never going to be a better time, trust me.

So, make sure that a copy of this book is in every room in the house, and in the back pocket of every family member. There should be one in every room you ever might be in, one in the fridge, one by the porn collection, one by the TV remote; you simply don't know where you'll be when the virus first strikes.

I hereby authorize you to make as many free copies of this book as you see fit to perform this function. Put them on Facebook, Tweet them to yourselves. Alert the whole human population of these simple rules.

Please note, dear human, I have written EIGHT separate Zombie Bible guides, and have included them ALL in this ONE publication. This is HUGE value for money. Please note I am NOT interested in money, the authors are both veritable Mother Theresa's and our only concern is saving your collective asses. And let's face it; if I don't save you, then at least maybe we'll have a better standard of zombie after the apocalypse. It's a win-win situation for everyone.

Guides included below are;

Normal Zombie Survival Guide

Children's Zombie Survival Guide

Pets Zombie Survival Guide

Grandparent's Zombie Survival Guide

Pregnant Mother's Zombie Survival Guide

Liberal's Zombie Survival Guide

Conservative's Zombie Survival guide

(All Guides included below at no extra charge.)

Zombie Foreword

Okay. You have to come to terms with the fact that you are a zombie, after 8 weeks, officially in the 99%. This book is targeted at you, and hopefully will lessen the chances of you being targeted by the hard sights of the laser-guided, gun-toting, lead-poisoning human 1%.

This book is intentionally short. It has to be. You're a zombie, for goodness sake; your attention span is shorter than a sparrow's pecker in a cold day in April.

(I do really apologize to the humans here, for the reason above, this book *has* to be short, don't blame my lack of forethought or ideas. It's not actually aimed at just you anyway, it's mostly aimed at the zombie you will undoubtedly become. When that time arrives, you'll thank me for being so concise, trust me.)

So, zombies, read this book, get those unused, grey synapses firing, and prepare for your survival.

Hopefully with this guide in your back pocket, you'll survive to the end to get the helicopter delivered vaccine. Just don't shuffle too close to the chopper blades in your excitement! We've all seen that movie clip.

BTW; this guide is also not rocket science; it's not intended as such. With your brains so much Swiss cheese, your skin the same undefinable color as a Frenchman's underpants, and smelling like a cross between Limburger and stale chicken salad left in a hot car, you guys couldn't do *first* grade science, so I'm keeping it simple.

Easy steps, in big letters, easy for your poor red, bloodshot, zombie eyes to read.

(Also; it was intended that an Audio book accompany the paperback, narrated by a comedian, trying to sound like the President, but he made a total hash of it, and sounded more like George Burns on crack, so we put a kybosh on that idea before we got sued. Our zombie lawyer isn't that good, and we don't want to overwork him.)

So, pause here, and go look in every room in the house. If you have performed the instructions back when you were a human, there should be one Zombie Bible in every room. For non-selfish zombies, please don't take the kids one. If you do, the kids will perish and you'll feel lonely when you get the vaccine, although you won't remember exactly why. If you can't find yours, use the Pregnant Mother's guide instead; it's almost the same. If you already have a pregnant mother in the house, no luck for you, and use the conservative's one. They have enough guns anyway, and probably have bought up all the available copies of this guide to keep them away from liberals.

If you can't find a Zombie bible anywhere, then one of two things have happened;

One; You've either NOT performed the instructions as a human when you first bought this guide, and are therefore an utter ass. (But in this instance all is not lost, you're reading it now, so must have just picked it up JUST as the zombie holocaust/apocalypse happened. Very coincidental.)

Or two; You're the most coincidental/fluk-ey/lucky guy on the planet, because the zombie holocaust/apocalypse is happening just as you open this book for the first time. Like the Jew said on "Monty Python's Life of Brian"…. "You Lucky Bastard."

THE ZOMBIE BIBLE; PART ONE

(FOR HUMANS BEFORE THE ZOMBIE HOLOCAUST)

REALIZING THAT YOUR ORIGINAL PLAN IS CRAP.

Firstly I'd like to start off by saying well done on taking the first steps to ensuring your survival in the Zombie Holocaust/Apocalypse.

You've never spent money so wisely in your life.

One of the best values for the cost of this guide recently for me was a single margarita. Now whilst being delicious, nutritious, and full of tequila, it didn't actually prepare me for the Holocaust, and gave me 1/10 of a sore head in the morning.

The other nine drinks had nothing to do with it.

The Zombie Bible;

The reason for writing the survival guide is threefold;

1. To get it into your thick post-Neanderthal modern skull that you have to make a plan.
2. To hammer into your thick post-Neanderthal modern skull that you actually have to go through with the plan.
3. To save your worthy ass whether you have or you haven't gone through with the plan; because you've spent your hard-earned cash with me, and I think your ass is worth something.

THE PLAN

(FOR HUMANS BEFORE THE ZOMBIE HOLOCAUST)

THE CHANCE OF SURVIVING THE INITIAL VIRUS

For many years I've been spreading the word that you've got to have a plan if you want to stay alive during/after the Zombie Uprising/Holocaust/Apocalypse.

(But here I must pause. This phrase, *Zombie Uprising/Holocaust/Apocalypse* is already getting old, so I thought I'd develop my own acronym. I tried over a hundred, but this is the best one;

Biological Infestation of Gene-pool, leading to Zombie Infection and Transformation.

B.I.G.Z.I.T.

That leaves the government with Operation B.I.G.Z.I.T. cleanup.

(If you can do better, email me! I will pay serious cash for the best one, I would even go all the up to $5.99 if it was really good.)

Anyway, it's been one of the quirks I've had, growing up, wondering where I'd be when BIGZIT happened.

My favorite place is in a huge paddling pool of baby oil, covered in naked lingerie models, all covered in the aforementioned baby oil.

(The biggest criteria here, of course, is the escape probabilities of the baby oil… The naked slippery zombie lingerie models would never be able to get their hands on me, I'd be SO slick. I'd escape SO easily….. and escape was the only thing on my mind in the visualization, trust me. If the actual holocaust didn't happen in the paddling pool, we'd just shrug our shoulders and go home for a quiet evening of Monopoly.)

Ok, you've read all the zombie books.

You've seen all the zombie movies, and zombie stuff on television.

You've even soaked up all the "after humans" documentaries.

You think you've got it all worked out.

But you haven't. Trust me.

You may have your 9mm, next to the porn and the baby oil, in your 'secret' place.

You may have a rendezvous site for the family.

(Well done for thinking that far ahead, few get this far.)

You may have stocks of fresh bottled water, and enough ammunition to kill China, or France, or at least put a dent in the nobility.

(Again, well done.)

But there's one thing you've missed.... Trust me. One thing you've not even considered.... You may get hit early. You may get turned into a zombie before you can even raise a limp middle finger in mock protest.

With enough stock of fresh spring bottled water in the basement to float the Bismarck, enough C-Rations to feed Manhattan, and enough ammunition to start world war four... you've over achieved.

(Again, Kudos to your forward thinking, but you've still not got my point.)

But what happens if the zombie virus, in all possibility created by the government's clandestine laboratory for unintended consequences (down the hall from the Roswell alien autopsy morgue) floats in your front door and hits your family head-on? 3 out of 4 of you are 'zombie toast' before you've even thought of grabbing your weapons.

Despite the best plans in the world, despite countless hours in bars with drunken plans laboriously written on napkins and beermats, you're screwed… FUBAR.

In fact to quote Tango and Cash, it's FUBAR- Big Time.

You've wasted all your valuable resources on water that some lucky bastard will drink, food that some fortunate dotard will eat, baby oil for someone else to revel in, and ammunition for someone else to try to kill you. You'd be as well spending your time writing your name on every bullet you own.

Now that sounds dumb, doesn't it?

I've watched all the zombie movies too, and sat through all the survival documentaries, and as soon as you are hit with the virus; you're a sudden inglorious statistic.

BLAMMO! You're a zombie! One of the shambling 75%.

Even if you survive the first wave…

BLAMMO! Eight weeks later, you're one of the world's statistics; one of the 99%, one of the shuffling masses waiting for the zombie Messiah to arrive.

You're free food for wild animals, and target practice for the 1% with laser-guided assault rifles. (Using the guns and ammunition from your secret place, and doing all kinds of nasty things with your stock of porn and baby oil!)

##Zombie Bible HAZE Stat## Three in four of mankind will be zombie-fied in the first stage of the spread of the virus. First Contact. 75%.

If you survive the first wave of infestation, (remaining human) and are driving in your car when it hits, think long and hard of the consequences.

Suddenly stopped in busy traffic, this means that the next three cars in front of you will be filled with shambling, shuffling predators, out for your blood and brains.

And you're canned up in your Prius, like a fresh tuna sandwich, waiting for lunch hour.

The 'lucky' 25% of the population at large have natural or other immunities which Hollywood never clearly defines, but undoubtedly, this is what the vaccine is developed from.

##Zombie Bible HAZE Stat## As civilization breaks down, another 10% will perish in the first week from accidents in the initial panic.

Looking for loved ones drives the surviving 25% of the human population utterly loopy. They'll try to cross the Red Sea in a peanut shell if they think they've got a chance of making it over. We're talking severely psychologically un-hinged individuals here; the kind of people that would cave your skull for a look at the map in your pocket, rather than ask for a peek.

So after the first week of the outbreak, we're already close to a 10% human survival rate.

And these are generous rates, I'll tell you. Some Hollywood movies have the *initial virus casualties* at 95%, not the generous HAZE 75%.

##Zombie Bible WIKI Stat## Depending on what time of day/week the initial wave of the virus hits, between 10 and 35% of the population will be displaced from their home base (and their porn, baby oil and ammunition).

This means 10-35% of survivors will be at their wits end, screaming into rapidly deadening cell phones, trying to get home to their loved ones. They will kill anything in their way, and if my statistics are correct, only 10% will actually be travelling home to human people.

Think of this for a moment.... 90% of the human survivors will be frenetic killing machines on their way home, killing everything in their paths, only to return home to an empty house, or to meet the new zombie family.

(**##Zombie Bible HAZE Stat##** The dubiety in any of the above percentages allows for a common inherent 'family' immunity to the initial outbreak, rather than just relying on normal statistical analysis.)

Anyway...

Even with the initial odds (75%) stacked against you, let's say you actually survive the first wave of the virus. Before you rush across town, or go downstairs to breakfast, you have a terrible conclusion to face up to.

##Zombie Bible HAZE Stat## You're a survivor, yes, but the chances of an immediate family member *also* surviving are less than 20%.

One in Five.

That makes the chance of a husband and wife team surviving; 4%.

Husband/wife/and one kid; 0.06%.

Think of that before you start off on your death defying rampage to get home.

If you're upstairs just getting your shoes on in the morning, and you hear the news on your small color television, I'd be pretty freaking careful going down to breakfast!

TRUST ME; WE BOTH KNOW YOU HAVE TO HAVE A PLAN. BUT THE PLAN HAS TO BE MORE ENCOMPASSING THAN THE ONE YOU ALREADY HAVE. YOU HAVE TO THINK OUTSIDE THE BOX, YOU HAVE TO MAKE YOUR PLAN FIT THE STATISTICAL TEMPLATE.

THE PLAN
(FOR HUMANS BEFORE THE ZOMBIE HOLOCAUST)
THE CHANCE OF SURVIVING THE CARNAGE THAT FOLLOWS

Okay. Let's take the unlikely situation that after the BIGZIT, you survive the initial virus.

Let's make the assumption that you have to get home. Find the wife. Find the kids. It's not likely, looking at statistics, but we know you've *GOT* to know either way.

Everyone does; it's human nature.

You have to rustle up whatever parts of the original plan you have left, and adapt it to the circumstances. You have to survive; and unless you've got the biggest NERF gun in the world, it's time for the killing to start.

Ever since a giant Galapagos turtle whispered in the ear of an Englishman called 'Chuck', 'survival of the fittest' has only been a catchphrase, but now, after the initial virus, it's become the law of the land. With 75% of the population now zombie freaks, and the other 25% freaking out; it's about to get pretty freaking ugly out there.

To get home, you have to pass obstacles. You have to overcome many adversaries, and for that you have to engage in some form of conflict.

Maiming won't do. A zombie will crawl across the grass at you when only his head remains, grabbing the green turf for traction with his teeth.

You have to learn to kill, just to get across town.

And I mean kill; head shot.

For food/gas/water, you have to kill some more. You have to kill both zombies AND humans. Admitted, that first one will be traumatic, but you may not have time to find yourself a greeting card with quite the right sentiment to capture your emotions, before you're forced to kill your second, third, fourth.

And kill you will, brave Jedi knight!

You have to be some cold, calculating bastard to do it with no thought of right and wrong. But you've got to be strong. Take the ethics arguments, the conscience battle, the human heartbreak.... and stash them in your "secret" place, next to the rest of your kinky paraphernalia and guns. Worship them at a later time, if it ever arrives.

In the first days after the initial virus, we've discussed above that a further 10% of the initial population will die, just through the violent carnage that will inevitably follow.

So you establish the fate of your immediate family.

You now have to find a secure shelter.

A shelter hopefully away from other groups with guns, also looking for a secure shelter. You already have details in your plan, trust me, just go look again. There it is, written in my own plan;

Initial Secure Shelter; Nearest Ikea Superstore.

But after the initial strike, you have to re-group, count your losses, re-organize.

You go back to your Zombie Holocaust/Apocalypse (BIGZIT) Plan. You've thought of food, guns, ammunition, water, baby oil… you've survived with one family member, you've got across town to reach them safely…. You've found a safe defensible place that no one else has found (Including zombies…. yet)… you're hunkered down, ready to defend it.

You think you're in the clear….

(And you could sit here for many days, secure in your invincibility)

But you don't see what's coming.

Because you CAN'T see what's coming.

It's invisible. Many millions of dead bodies litter the streets and homes.

The microbes come calling; Cholera, Typhoid, Diphtheria, Dysentery, Food Poisoning. Then, getting progressively bigger; Small Insects, Bigger Insects, Mice, Rats, Wild Cats and Dogs, Other Wild animals, Hippies with VW Microbuses, and other, unprepared, desperate survivors.

You now need a stock of medical supplies that you'd never ever considered, even if you had a GREAT plan to begin with.

So…. Off you go to get the newly needed medical supplies, and your group gets hit by other groups, all trying to get those 'essential' supplies.

Your survivors return to your secret, safe place, and wait some more, getting complacent.

Then, after you think you're in the clear….

The virus strikes again.

##Zombie Bible WIKI Stat## In 1918, at the end of the First World War, a flu virus struck worldwide. The "Spanish" flu killed an estimated 50-300 million people, and infected over 500 million (27% of the planet's population).

The first wave did most of the killing, but there were at least SIX mutated versions of the flu in subsequent months. The secondary flus killed another estimated 10 million people before they eventually fizzled out.

So, the mutated zombie virus will strike the already weakened population.

Again, and again, each time turning more of the human survivors into the dreaded un-dead.

##Zombie Bible HAZE Stat## Pretty freaking quick, we're down to the 'fabled' 1% survival rate after just eight short weeks.

Pause for breath here, the average human has 11 close friends, and knows 36 people intimately as 'good friends'. He knows 167 workmates, and 519 acquaintances.

That's 700 plus. You're now down to 7.

SO…

After 8 weeks you have a 1% chance of human (non-zombie) survival.

After 8 weeks; A surviving husband and wife pair; less than 0.02%. (One chance in ten thousand)

After 8 weeks; A husband/wife/one kid….

Less than one chance in three million.

Like I said before; YOU HAVE TO HAVE A PLAN…. AND THE PLAN HAS TO BE MORE ENCOMPASSING THAN THE ONE YOU ALREADY HAVE.

(I'd like to write this next bit in HUGE letters, but I'm limited by the size of this book. After all it has to fit in your back pocket.)

STATISTICALLY; YOUR PLAN HAS TO BE; SURVIVING THE HOLOCAUST AS A ZOMBIE.

Because that's what you or most of your family will be.

YOU HAVE TO SURVIVE AS A ZOMBIE TILL THE HELICOPTERS ARRIVE, AND DISTRIBUTE THE VACCINE.

AND YOU HAVE TO BE IN GOOD ENOUGH SHAPE AS A ZOMBIE TO SURVIVE THE TRANSFORMATION BACK TO HUMANITY.

That's a tall order.

When to start? NOW! While you are human, and can still *make* plans.

THE PLAN

(FOR HUMANS BEFORE THE ZOMBIE HOLOCAUST)

Plain statistics…

THE CHANCE OF SURVIVING AS A HUMAN

Less than 1%. (Nuff said)

THE CHANCE OF SURVIVING AS A ZOMBIE

Greater than 50%. (E-Nuff said, surely.)

I'm going to explain the 50% figure, as I'm being VERY generous here.

For 50% of the zombie population to be destroyed beyond the help of a vaccine, a LOT of them will have to deteriorate/be killed.

300 million people in the USA. 1% human survivor rate.

For 50% of the zombie population to be incapacitated beyond the help of vaccine, the survivors have to kill/maim 149.5 million zombies.

Even if you had enough ammunition, we're talking a heck of a lot of killing time. That's 100 zombies for every surviving human.

That's a very tall figure.

THE PLAN

(FOR HUMANS BEFORE THE ZOMBIE HOLOCAUST)

THE CHANCE OF SURVIVING TILL THE VACCINE ARRIVES

As we've seen, the chances of a zombie surviving to the end and getting the vaccine are significantly greater than those of a surviving human.

Now….

I've read all the books. (They're in the 'Zombie Apocalypse' rucksack for future reference)

I've got my 'escape from the city' planned. (Car is always fully loaded with gas/petrol)

I know our rendezvous point. (The nearest Ikea store… don't ask, old story)

My weapons are arranged by ease of gathering and effectiveness. (Ammunition checked weekly)

I've even got names of my 'alpha' survival group. (Based on a chart of 'effectiveness' in a fight; golfers and baseball players finally prove their worth!)

Chris; Golfer. Good at close range with a Taylormade driver, and his dad's got an ex WW2 Luger pistol.

Danny; Golfer. He owns a Ping set, two shotguns and a Landrover.

David; Geek. But very handy with a baseball bat; he's been playing his WII a heck of a lot, and he's hit each of us at least once, and cracked a fish tank. I'd back him in a one-to-one fight with a 'shambler' anyday.

Tony; Good looking guy (Lorraine's pick.... Saying nothing) All in all, pretty useless, but I can run faster than him, so I don't care that much.

Sandra; (my pick.... Saying *absolutely* nothing). She actually doesn't *know* she's in my survival group, but she works in the local Tesco, and lives opposite my house. I've seen through the curtains a couple of times, and I'm not leaving without grabbing her.

Helen; she's fencer. Not the sword type, she actually puts up fences, and has two (TWO) battery powered nail-guns.

Oh, and Jane. She owns a Hummer, and is very handy, just round the corner. And did I mention; she owns a Hummer; the zombie fighting vehicle of choice.

Hummer actually knew this when they named the vehicle; HUMMER stands for;

Huge Undead Monster Mashing Escape Route.

(An amazing acronym, you must admit)

Anyway; my list has all been communicated, emailed, Facebooked, or lectured, to my loved ones. (We know the phone system will fail first).

Pesky cow-orkers (No, that wasn't a typo) and irritating in-laws, bosses, neighbors, and the guy across the street who plays his music too loud when he's drunk, have all been given intentionally false information, so as to become unwitting decoys for our brilliant escape to the nearest Ikea Store.

WE HAVE A PLAN. EVERYONE SHOULD DO.

But then it finally hits you….. all these plans will collapse totally as your friends are caught unawares, out of town, away from home, hit by virus, diverted by other, more pressing, personal needs. (Such as shagging the overtly delicious babysitter, Sandra opposite, Lorraine's Tony, or the painfully hard-bodied life-guard at the local pool, or all at the same time…. with lots of baby oil.)

But listen to what I've been trying to tell say; you probably won't survive. No matter how much you plan, the chances of being in the last handful of survivors that makes it out of the city and form your own community are slim to none.

If you want to survive, you need to rethink your strategy. There's no point in making plans with people for the zombie end…. If they don't turn up, through no fault of yours, your plan is screwed.

Only one in ten of your list will make it to the rendezvous.

So if you don't team up with friends, are you going to trust complete strangers?

Of course you are. Because you're going to have to!

I mean, you've got the plan, water, guns, food, ammunition…. And you're going to give it away to complete strangers? That just sounds dumb. Right?

Why align yourself with a small ragtag group of survivors when you will probably get infected in the first wave of the uprising or on your way to your 'safe' zone (Ikea here we come).

All it takes is one unlucky bite, one wrong stumble or just being outnumbered by a shuffling mass of the undead and straight away, it’s game over.

LET’S FACE IT… HOWEVER WELL THOUGHT THROUGH YOU THOUGHT IT WAS; YOUR PLAN IS CRAP.

YOU’RE PLANNING TO SAVE UP YOUR MONEY, BUY STUFF, THEN JUST GIVE AWAY YOUR STUFF FOR PEOPLE TO KILL YOU WITH? THAT SOUNDS DUMB.

So it’s time to make a plan B. If you can’t beat em, you gotta join em. Only problem now is that part of surviving as a zombie means you’ve got to try to stay alive (or should that be un-dead) when your food is trying to kill you.

That’s where this book comes in. I'll show you how to survive, or at least outlive all those other brain dead morons who didn’t have the foresight to plan properly or correctly calculate their own survival chances.

AS A ZOMBIE.

THE ZOMBIE BIBLE; PART TWO

SURVIVING AS A ZOMBIE

ZOMBIE GUIDE STEP 1

GET/BUY/STEAL A THICK BLACK SHARPIE

(Magic Marker, Permanent Marker, etc, etc)

Okay; in case of Zombie Holocaust/Apocalypse (BIGZIT: Biological Infestation of Gene-pool, leading to Zombie Infection and Transformation) you need a black Sharpie in your pocket. You need this from day 1 of reading this guide. Keep a black Sharpie in every pocket, and handbag you own **AT ALL TIMES**. Check them weekly to see if they work. A black Sharpie will keep you alive after the zombie apocalypse; trust me.

Feel your pocket right now. There should be a black Sharpie there.

Congratulations! You've completed the first step in surviving the zombie apocalypse; THE THICK BLACK SHARPIE.

If you DO NOT have a black Sharpie in your pocket; steal one from the wife, the kids, the mother in law.

So….

YOU SHOULD NOW HAVE A BLACK SHARPIE IN YOUR POCKET (If not, go back to ZOMBIE STEP 1.)

ZOMBIE STEP 2

GET/BUY/STEAL A WIDE ROLL OF CELLOTAPE

(Clear Tape, Scotch Tape, etc, etc)

Okay; in case of BIGZIT: Biological Infestation of Gene-pool, leading to Zombie Infection and Transformation (Zombie Holocaust/Apocalypse) you need a roll of wide Cellotape in your pocket. You need this from day 1 of reading this guide. Keep a roll of wide Cellotape in your pocket at all times. Don't worry about it sticking out. You can feel superior when you see some guy without one.

Feel your pocket right now. There should be a wide roll of Cellotape there.

Congratulations! You've completed the second step in surviving the zombie apocalypse; THE WIDE ROLL OF CELLOTAPE.

If you DO NOT have a wide roll of Cellotape in your pocket; steal one from work, from school, Staples or any other major office accessory outlet.

So….

YOU SHOULD NOW HAVE A BLACK SHARPIE AND A WIDE ROLL OF CELLOTAPE IN YOUR POCKET (If not, go back to ZOMBIE STEP 2.)

ZOMBIE STEP 3

THE ZOMBIE CARD

Okay; in case of BIGZIT, you need to get the Zombie Card printed. And do it pretty fricking quick.

The card is below, is just exactly what you need.

Get it photocopied and printed out, or make your own.

Humans; photocopy one for each member of the family.

Selfless zombies; photocopy it. Selfish zombies; cut it out.

Okay, you don't need to run to a mirror; here's what it says;

"Don't panic. You're a Zombie. Look in your back pocket. There's a book. OPEN IT AT PAGE ONE"

If this is before the BIGZIT/Zombie Holocaust/Apocalypse, take your copy of the card, and laminate it.

Put it in your pocket next to your black Sharpie and your wide roll of Cellotape.

Feel your pocket right now. There should be a black Sharpie, a wide roll of Cellotape and a laminated card there.

Congratulations! You've completed the third step in surviving the zombie apocalypse; THE THICK BLACK SHARPIE, THE WIDE ROLL OF CELLOTAPE, AND THE LAMINATED ZOMBIE CARD.

If you DO NOT have a laminated card in your pocket; steal one from the wife, the kids, the mother in law. Or in the absence of other zombies to prey on, read on. We'll teach you to make your own Zombie Card.

So….

YOU SHOULD NOW HAVE A BLACK SHARPIE, A WIDE ROLL OF CELLOTAPE, AND A LAMINATED CARD IN YOUR POCKET (If not, go back to ZOMBIE STEP 3.)(OR READ ON, WHATEVER)

ZOMBIE STEP 4

THE HAMMER AND BELT CLIP

(For everyone)

Yup, everyone, even you, chump-change; the guy that reckons he's so freaking good at survival, that he'll make it to be the last human on the planet. BTW, have fun with that, because if the vaccine hasn't been developed by then, then you'll have to develop one! So get off your skinny gun-toting ass and start enrolling in pharmaceutical college. You've not thought this through enough, and I've had to do the thinking for you! And you thought you had a plan!

In most countries in the world, there are laws against the carrying of guns and knives, but NOT against the carrying of a hammer. Even in non-zombie fights, a hammer is a pretty good weapon against a knife anyway, so this should be part of EVERY survival guide, not just the zombie ones.

Anyway, back to the hammer and belt clip.

Okay; in case of BIGZIT, you need a hammer on your belt.

(Check your hip. If there's a hammer already clipped to your belt, go on to ZOMBIE STEP 5. Unless you've forgotten your numbers already, then just read on, don't let it upset you.)

(Use the black Sharpie in your pocket and complete this next line yourself with the exact location of your hammer and belt clip)

MY HAMMER AND BELT CLIP IS IN

…………………………………………………………..

(Garage, tool box, kitchen drawer, etc etc)

Replace the black Sharpie back into your pocket.

Time for small celebration?

If a location is ALREADY written above in black Sharpie, then pat yourself on the back. You actually read this guide when you first got it.

Check your belt; if you feel a hammer, then pat yourself on the back again, you actually went through with it, bought a hammer and belt clip, then didn't use it for some household chore and not return it to its proper place. Man, you're good!

In case of Zombie Apocalypse….. get hammer….. clip to belt.

Now, here the gun-toting survivor is going to say; "My belt is already crammed with guns, pistols, crossbows, and knives! I got no room for a hammer!"

Punko- listen up and listen good.

If you have all that crap on your belt, and you survive the apocalypse as a human, that's fantastic. But, honey-brain, the odds are against it. Okay, you may be one of the lucky ones who survive the initial outbreak of the virus, but, chances are you'll make a mistake, and you'll be a zombie one day.

Then what?

Then you'll eventually pick all those things off your belt, look at them longingly, wondering what the heck they're for, and drop them with a shake of the head to the ground. The human silently following behind you, picking up your discarded weapons, will grin widely, pick up the gun and shoot your brains out from behind.

You've just provided your murderer with his murder weapon. And you thought you had a plan?

You need a hammer. Trust me.

This is the whole idea of this book…. ***You have to make plans for being a zombie***. This puts you at the top of the zombie survival chain, and you'll be the first zombie to get the vaccine at the end.

Feel your pocket right now. There should be a black Sharpie, a wide roll of Cellotape, and a laminated zombie card. Touch your hammer; it should be right there, where you left it, on your belt clip.

Congratulations! You've completed the first four steps in surviving the zombie apocalypse; THE BLACK SHARPIE, WIDE ROLL OF CELLOTAPE, THE LAMINATED ZOMBIE CARD, AND THE HAMMER AND BELT CLIP.

If at this stage you have no hammer at your side, then steal one. Take the initiative, for goodness sake, it's not rocket science!

(I'll wait here while you return from the local hardware store, or next door's garden shed)

So….

YOU SHOULD NOW HAVE A BLACK SHARPIE, A WIDE ROLL OF CELLOTAPE, AND A LAMINATED ZOMBIE CARD

IN YOUR POCKET AND A HAMMER CLIPPED TO YOUR BELT! (If not, go back to ZOMBIE STEP 4.)

ZOMBIE STEP 5

THE ZOMBIE BIBLE

Okay; in case of BIGZIT, you need a copy of this book in your back pocket.

So, this step is easy. Buy a copy for every member of the household. ALWAYS have yours in your back pocket.

If this is the first time you're reading the 'Zombie Bible', then go buy another copy right now. You need one in the back of your pocket just in case the zombie holocaust/apocalypse happens as you're reading this book.

Think about it; you're reading the Zombie Bible, the Government accidentally-released virus sprays through your open window, and you forget what you're doing. You stare at the book in your hand, then shake your head in confusion, and let it fall to the bathroom floor…. You're lost to me, and your chance of surviving the zombie holocaust/apocalypse has just decreased a hundred fold. All because you didn't buy another copy, and put it in your back pocket?

Don't want to pay for two copies? How can you put a price on survival?

So…. go buy it…. Now…. While you are still human enough to work the remember where the bookstore is.

Congratulations! You've completed the first five steps in surviving the zombie apocalypse; THE BLACK SHARPIE, THE WIDE ROLL OF CELLOTAPE, THE LAMINATED CARD, THE HAMMER and THE ZOMBIE BIBLE.

If at this stage, you DON'T have a copy of this book in your back pocket, I'm shocked and stunned; you're just not looking after yourself properly! No one can be this stupid. However, if you are a zombie, and you've forgotten where the bookstore is; just go outside and find the first unsuspecting zombie with a 'Zombie Bible' in his pocket, and steal it. Don't worry, everyone will have one, trust me. And he won't notice his being stolen…. He's a zombie.

So….

YOU SHOULD NOW HAVE A BLACK SHARPIE, A WIDE ROLL OF CELLOTAPE, AND A LAMINATED CARD IN YOUR POCKET, A HAMMER CLIPPED TO YOUR BELT, AND A ZOMBIE BIBLE IN YOUR BACK POCKET! (If not, go back to ZOMBIE STEP 5 and repeat till done!)

ZOMBIE STEP 6

THE ZOMBIE FAILSAFE.

(For everyone)

Okay; in case of BIGZIT; Look at the back of your hands. If there is a message in black sharpie, saying “Look in a Mirror!”, and you can’t remember how it got there, I’ve got some bad news for you. You’re either suffering from a HUGE practical joke by your drunken mates last night…. Or you’re a Zombie.

If there is a message in black Sharpie, saying “Look in a Mirror!”, then guess what you should do?

GO TO A MIRROR! LOOK AT ALREADY-MENTIONED MIRROR!

You may be surprised to see a post-it note Cellotaped to your forehead.

If the note reads; *“Don’t panic. You’re a Zombie. Look in your back pocket. There’s a book. OPEN IT AT PAGE ONE”*

Then go directly to step 7.

(It’s down below, trust me. Zombies still having problems with numbers, just read on. Zombies having problems with simple instructions; go outside and find a speeding bullet with your head; oh, I forgot you can’t understand irony. How sad.)

Okay, if you’re still here with me, there’s no message on the back of your hands, or you’re too stupid to read instructions.

For those humans too stupid to read instructions, I'm going to ignore you. I take back what I said earlier; you're not worth the money you spent on this survival guide.

Okay, so there's NO message in black Sharpie, on the back of both hands, saying "Look in a Mirror!"? You need to write it yourself, right now.

Yes, I said YOU have to write it. Take the aforementioned Black Sharpie, and write in big letters on the back of BOTH hands; "Look in the Mirror!"

(I'll wait till you do this.)

(I'm also making the assumption that you still have both hands attached to your body. If you don't, go outside and be food for someone. When the vaccine arrives, they won't give it to you first anyway, you're way down on the pecking order. They know you won't survive the trauma back to humanity with only one arm, a profusely bleeding socket, and a lack of nurses to treat you.)

I digress.

Right, messages written, right? On the back of both hands?

The reason why I'm saying BOTH HANDS is pretty obvious for most zombie fans. But for the slow out there, and the zombie slow, we need to write it on the back of BOTH HANDS in case you lose one. Zombie limbs are easily bitten, wrenched, and cut off. There's no point in not being safe. It's like the Irishman who wears two condoms when having sex… in a suitably leprechaun accent, he says; "To be sure, to be sure."

(The bored reader might wonder why I'm being so pedantic about this, and methodical to the point of being boring… don't question the method when I'm teaching you to survive! Many people have already ignored me, and they're dead! Or un-dead. Whatever.)

Right. Look in your pocket for the laminated zombie card. If you don't have one, you have to make your own. Follow the instructions… (Those with a zombie card, just smile at your pre-planning smugness.)

For zombies, don't fret, just read the words really slowly.

To make your own zombie card…

Take a post-it note. The biggest one you can find. If you can't find a post it note, then paper will do. About the size of a playing card is perfect.

(Try and find a kind of dirty grey card, about the same color as your skin. This card will be placed on your forehead, if you use white card, it's just a target for the 1% with guns.)

(Okay, you may think I'm being cruel here, but actually it's a zombie aptitude test; those who use a grey card will survive, therefore the population will gravitate to be more intelligent…. (A reference to those Galapagos/Chuck conversations) Let's face it, these vaccines could take a few years to arrive.)

Back to the zombie card.

Write in clear letters in black Sharpie, write it again and again till the message comes through the back. Make sure you can read the letters from the back. They need to be clear.

(This why I suggest you do this whilst still human, this reverse letter thing takes a lot of understanding, and may not be easy for some zombies.)

The message on the post-it note should read;

"Don't panic. You're a Zombie. Look in your back pocket. There's a book. OPEN IT AT PAGE ONE"

Okay. Place the post-it note on a flat surface and turn it so that the writing is now face down.

It should now look like this;

Right, lay your laminated card or post-it note on the table.

Take the roll of Cellotape and stick it on the post-it note. Put the note onto your forehead, and look up into the mirror.

It should read correctly! Trust me, or if you're reading this for the first time, go use a mirror.

(The idea of thousands of people standing in their bathrooms, with a piece of my book on their foreheads does make me chuckle!)

Anyway….

If it does read correctly, roll tape round head, to fix it in place. Make sure you do this properly.

Okay. Look at yourself. Yes, you look like a twat zombie, but you're going to be one of those surviving twat zombies, so shut up and deal with it.

The message on your forehead should now read;

"Don't panic. You're a Zombie. Look in your back pocket. There's a book. OPEN IT AT PAGE ONE"

Congratulations! You've completed the first six steps in surviving the zombie apocalypse; THE BLACK SHARPIE, THE WIDE ROLL OF CELLOTAPE, THE LAMINATED ZOMBIE CARD, THE HAMMER, THE ZOMBIE BIBLE, and THE ZOMBIE FAILSAFE.

So….

YOU SHOULD NOW HAVE A BLACK SHARPIE IN YOUR POCKET, A HAMMER CLIPPED TO YOUR BELT, A ZOMBIE BIBLE IN YOUR BACK POCKET, AND A CELLOTAPED BAND ROUND YOUR HEAD WITH A MESSAGE ON IT SAYING; *"Don't panic. You're a Zombie. Look in your back pocket. There's a book. OPEN IT AT PAGE ONE"*

(If not, go back to ZOMBIE STEP 6 and try again!)

Notes on the Zombie Failsafe;

The zombie failsafe card on the forehead will save your life.

"But I'm not a zombie yet!" I hear you humans squeal....

If you're not a zombie, you're a human survivor, you've got to go out into the mad, bad world and get food, find loved ones, get somewhere safe. Right?

This is where the Zombie Failsafe comes into its own....

IF YOU DON'T MAKE A MISTAKE; you're in complete disguise with the rest of zombie kind. I anticipate selling a few billion of these books, so you'll be in concert with the rest of humanity.

IF YOU MAKE A MISTAKE; so, you're outside with that ridiculous Cellotape headband and laminated card/post-it note message on your forehead. The chances are you are going to make a mistake. My zombie apocalypse movie/tv survey shows that over 99% of human survivors get turned into zombies, either through the initial virus, or by zombie conversion. Think of the headband now, and how it'll save your life till the vaccine arrives.

When you make that mistake.... and you will.......

(This next visualization is far funnier if you think of Simon Pegg (From 'Shaun of the Dead') doing this.... Trust me.)

After you make your fatal mistake.... when you wake up later as a zombie, you'll eventually look at the message on the back of your hands, and this scene will unfold.....

"Duh? I can't think very good. But there's a message on the back of my hands, saying "*Look in the Mirror*!"." You give a little quixotic zombie pause, then perhaps have the crazy idea…. "Hey, maybe I should look in the mirror." So you toddle off looking for a mirror. Even if you get distracted, you'll eventually read the message on the back of your hands so often, you'll get the idea to look in a mirror. Then, in the mirror, you'll see your own crazy zombie face for the first time…. (You won't panic, you're a zombie, zombies are not known for their panicking properties, but you might get a little melancholic. But there's a message on your forehead….. that piques your zombie curiosity…. you lean closer to the mirror and WAMMO!

The message on the post-it note reads; *"Don't panic. You're a Zombie. Look in your back pocket. There's a book. OPEN IT AT PAGE ONE"*

Again, there's a curious expression flitting over your features (You've seen it in all the zombie movies; that quiet zombie WTF moment, when the penny drops in the dark recesses of the zombie mind, and a synapse connection is made. You've just had a zombie Homer Simpson moment!) and you reach round to your back pocket, and find a book there…. You take it out, and look at it. It says;

The Zombie Bible: a Zombie Guide to Surviving the Holocaust

(Living as a zombie, and surviving to the end when a vaccine is delivered)

By Ian Hall & Lorraine James

You're intrigued, and you open the book. Captivated, you begin to read the guide, and somehow the ideas inside enable you to survive to the end. You'll get the vaccine, I've saved your life, and you'll be eternally grateful.

So, on with your survival.

ZOMBIE STEP 7

SAVING THE FAMILY; PART 1; THE KIDS

Okay; in case of Zombie Holocaust/Apocalypse, you need to perform the last six steps BEFORE helping someone else in your household. It's a bit like putting on your own oxygen mask in an airplane as it's crashing; you need to do your own BEFORE you attend to help the wife and kids.

Now, you help the kids.

You can use the following Template, I'm sure it's self-explanatory. Blow it up to full page size.

DEAR.................................

(Insert own name above for future use)

Despite its horrible disfigurement

This is actually one of your kids!

PLEASE DO NOT EAT OR MAIM

Signed.................................

(Sign above in black Sharpie, and laminate)

Whilst still in human state, please laminate the above. Make as many copies as you have kids. Make the kids carry these everywhere they go, even to school. Make another copy to hang in their bedroom.

There's a 30% chance the Zombie Holocaust/Apocalypse will arrive when they're in bed.

In case of Zombie Holocaust/Apocalypse; use the wide roll of Cellotape to tape it to the kid's chest.

SAVING THE FAMILY; PART 2; THE HUSBAND/WIFE/BOY-GIRLFRIEND/SIGNIFICANT OTHER

In case of Zombie Holocaust/Apocalypse, having saved/fail-safed yourself and your kids, you must now turn to the partner.

(It must be stressed right here, that this is a wonderful time to sever ties, if you're so inclined. I'm not advocating mass separation here, but, you know, if you're teetering, this is the time to say "Cowabunga Dude!" and skip this step and go direct to; SAVING THE FAMILY; PART 4; THE EXTRA FOODGROUPS.)

For those still wishing to continue their present relationship, please use the template below, again, self-explanatory.

DEAR.............................
(Insert own name above for future use.)

Despite my endearing zombie crusts
I'm the one you will be trying to hump
when the vaccine eventually comes
HANDS OFF; LEAVE MY PARTS INTACT
THIS NOTICE IS FOR YOUR OWN
GOOD, AS WELL AS MY OWN

Signed;..

Ask partner to sign it, then again, laminate, and use wide roll of Cellotape to tape this notice round his/her middle.

SAVING THE FAMILY; PART 3; YOURSELF

Okay; in case of Zombie Holocaust/Apocalypse, you need to think outside the box to survive.

You don't know your partner's deepest thoughts of you. You don't know the best way to trigger a survival reaction in him/her. You also don't know which zombies you'll be standing next to, so what do you write on your own billboard?

I've thought of it extensively, and here's my best shot;

Here's your own template, again, self-explanatory;

Yes, you have seen me before.

I'm a Movie Star.

If I get to the end of this
Zombie Holocaust/Apocalypse
I'm going to be SO grateful to you
I might even split my millions with you

PS; also great in bed, and resourceful.

I tried many differing ideas, but this was best, in general.

SAVING THE FAMILY; PART 4; THE OTHER FOODGROUPS

Okay; in case of Zombie Holocaust/Apocalypse, we need to apportion some sense of survival into your nice girly-type brain.

Humans are food. Nearby humans are easy food. Direct family aside, we have to sever ties with the more distant family titles.

For mother, father, aunt, uncle, niece, nephew etc, etc, etc….. Substitute one word; food.

For policeman, next-door-neighbor, cute girl at the cash register…... Substitute one word; food.

You won't remember them after the vaccine, so get it over with now.

Congratulations! You've completed the first seven steps in surviving the zombie apocalypse; THE BLACK SHARPIE, THE WIDE ROLL OF CELLOTAPE, THE LAMINATED ZOMBIE CARD, THE HAMMER, THE ZOMBIE BIBLE, THE ZOMBIE FAILSAFE, AND THERE'S LAMINATED OR HANDMADE NOTICES ON ALL YOUR IMMEDIATE FAMILY'S CHESTS.

So….

YOU SHOULD NOW HAVE A BLACK SHARPIE, AND THE WIDE ROLL OF CELLOTAPE IN YOUR POCKET, A HAMMER CLIPPED TO YOUR BELT, A ZOMBIE BIBLE IN YOUR BACK POCKET, A CELLOTAPED BAND ROUND YOUR HEAD WITH A MESSAGE ON IT SAYING; *"Don't panic. You're a Zombie. Look in your back pocket. There's a book. OPEN IT AT PAGE ONE"*

AND THERE'S LAMINATED OR HANDMADE NOTICES ON ALL YOUR IMMEDIATE FAMILY'S CHESTS. (If not, go back to ZOMBIE STEP 7 and try again!)

Zombies, feel smug. Feel very smug.

ZOMBIE STEP 8

THE QUICK DRAW

Okay; in case of Zombie Holocaust/Apocalypse we need to perfect the zombie quick draw.

This means, you look at the back of one of your hands, you see the writing, you go to a mirror, you see the sign, you look in your pocket, and you take out the Zombie Bible.

It's that easy.

If you've ever seen a western/cowboy movie/film, you may have marveled at the quick, instinctive reactions of the gunslingers. They achieve this by practice.

We're going to do this right now. Practice.

Practice makes perfect, and we're trying to survive, so we have to be good. Real good.

(Human's ignore this part, this is going to be quite bizarre enough without giving instructions to both species)

Zombies; think;

BACK OF HAND. BACK OF HAND. BACK OF HAND. BACK OF HAND. BACK OF HAND.

You have to concentrate…

BACK OF HAND. BACK OF HAND. BACK OF HAND. BACK OF HAND. BACK OF HAND.

Now close the book and put it in your back pocket.

Okay, well it was nice knowing you. To those who left the book at this stage, sorry, you didn't make the cut. You're now dwindling in numbers like goodly virgins in a pirate brothel.

Galapagos/Chuck moment.

To those of you who re-join me here…… well done.

Really; well done.

Congratulations! You've completed the first EIGHT steps in surviving the zombie apocalypse; THE BLACK SHARPIE, THE WIDE ROLL OF CELLOTAPE, THE LAMINATED ZOMBIE CARD, THE HAMMER, THE ZOMBIE BIBLE, THE ZOMBIE FAILSAFE, and THE ZOMBIE MEMORY TEST.

So….

YOU SHOULD NOW HAVE A BLACK SHARPIE, A WIDE ROLL OF CELLOTAPE AND A LAMINATED CARD IN YOUR POCKET, A HAMMER CLIPPED TO YOUR BELT, A ZOMBIE BIBLE IN YOUR BACK POCKET, AND A CELLOTAPED BAND ROUND YOUR HEAD WITH A MESSAGE ON IT SAYING; *"Don't panic. You're a Zombie. Look in your back pocket. There's a book. OPEN IT AT PAGE ONE",* AND THERE'S LAMINATED OR HANDMADE NOTICES ON ALL YOUR IMMEDIATE FAMILY'S CHESTS.

AND….. YOU'VE PASSED THE MEMORY TEST 'QUICK DRAW'.

The more times you actually do STEP 8, the easier it will become. I think.

This is not an exact science.

THE ZOMBIE BIBLE; PART THREE

EVERY-DAY DEALING WITH BEING A ZOMBIE

ZOMBIE STEP 9

LET'S MAKE SURE YOU *ARE* A ZOMBIE, NOT JUST A COUCH POTATO

Okay; in case of Zombie Holocaust/Apocalypse, you have to know for sure, don't you?

Let's face it, you've done so well that by now you may be getting the idea that you're NOT a zombie. Right?

I mean, lots of species just roll around the house, not doing much; nerds, computer geeks, fat dads, fat moms (think of Gilbert Grape) etc, etc

Let me tell you. Normal people have given up reading long before now. The Zombie Bible copies are in every room, maybe months, years ago. They've forgotten all about them. The readers are probably zombies by now. Let's face it, most people will be… eventually.

This is the aim of this guide (Like I've said before); to take you through the shock of being a zombie, and make sure you survive to the end when a vaccine is developed.

Okay, you've survived the initial holocaust, and not sure how to carry on, huh?

You've got one question to ask yourself; What's the title of this book?

It's a simple question, I've mentioned it often enough.

If you had to look back to the title to remember, I'm so sorry; you're probably a Zombie.

At this stage, I'm reminded of the; "You might be a Red-neck" series of jokes by Jeff Foxworthy. I sure think there's a few "You might be a Zombie" jokes out there, but perhaps that's another book.

Perhaps that's another career?

So… Are you a zombie? Well?

Let's establish that fact before going any further, shall we? If you can answer "yes" to any of the following questions, just stop reading, go directly back and do STEPS 1 THRU 7, and then put this book in your back pocket. (It's been ergonomically designed to fit there, don't worry.) You're not a zombie, and you passed this scientifically calibrated exam.

Have you had milk with your cereal in the last seven days?

Have you drank anything apart from blood in the last 7 days?

Have you eaten anything apart from flesh in the last 7 days?

Does the idea of tearing someone's arm off and having a damn good feed make you feel bad?

Okay, now remember, if you answered 'yes' to any of the questions, go back and do STEPS 1 THRU 7, then put the book in your back pocket.

Hi there….

If you're reading this part for the first time now, you're a zombie. You have to come to terms with this, and there are things you need to do to survive.

Don't get killed by the non-zombie survivors.

Find food. (Clean, healthy food. Vaccines can't fix poison.)

Find safety.

Not lose all your limbs (Even the best vaccine can't fix that!)

Now, there are things you have to accept.

You can't run. Your best speed is a well gaited shuffle.

You can't dodge a bullet.

You are IN DIRECT COMPETITION other zombies for the available human food.

You are the scourge of the planet, and target practice for the surviving human 1%.

But there is one significant thing to remember; you are also 99% of the population.

ZOMBIE STEP 10

FINDING ZOMBIE FOOD

Okay; in case of BIGZIT, humans are food, and you need to eat. You have to keep your strength up, or a vaccine will not help you. No matter how hungry you get, how desperate, try not to eat other zombies too much; you have no idea what they have (disease wise) and no idea where they've been. So, let's look at your other, non-zombie food sources.

Humans are food. (But there's only 1% left, so eat sparingly, and one of them might be the one who goes on to develop the vaccine!)

##Zombie Bible HAZE Stat## Facing zombie food facts; after BIGZIT there are still 3 million humans in the USA, that's a lot of zombie food. But there's 299,999,999 competing with you for every morsel of it.

Pets are food. (Be a pet lover, then after the apocalypse, stick them in the closet for later.)

##Zombie Bible WIKI Stat## 3 million humans; but there are 78 million dogs and 86 million cats in the USA. Over 1 million are in dog/cat pounds or in pet stores. So be a pet lover; get along to your local pet store and have a bite to eat! Taiwan's been cooking dogs for years, and so has your local Chinese restaurant… you KNOW they have, you just refuse to come to terms with the fact.)

##Zombie Bible WIKI Stat## Animals are food. Cows have much more meat on their bones than the average pussy, and I would much rather have a lean sirloin strip than a cat testicle any day! Horses have been a delicacy in France for years.

In Mexico they eat Armadillo.

The countryside abounds with wildlife, just ready to eat.

##Zombie Bible WIKI Stat## The USA wild deer population is estimated at 50 million. 1 million deer/car accidents happen in the USA every year. Antelope numbers are around 400,000. So you Ted Nugent zombies…. Get on out there. Herd them up!

##Zombie Bible WIKI Stat## In the USA there are 1 million dairy cows, 100 million beef cattle, 50 million sheep, 4 million goats, 10 million horses.

##Zombie Bible WIKI Stat## Above, we've estimated that there's close to 600 million other sources of fresh food out there that are NOT trying to kill you back!

600 million things you can eat that the other zombies haven't even considered. This book is trying to make you the leading alpha-zombie, let me lead you by the hand.

No animal is going to develop the vaccine…. Never! So eat animals first!

OTHER ANIMALS

If you live in the country, sheep, cows, goats and to a degree horses, are relatively docile. Some may come to you, thinking you're a friend, and a swing of your hammer will maim them enough to get your teeth into flesh. Remember to clip your hammer back on your belt before eating.

Horses; watch those hooves.... Unless you're French, of course, in which case you've got it coming, survival of the fittest and all, remember? Galapagos/Chuck?

In general, my own experience indicates that I would tend to dodge dogs and cat unless they're totally friendly; their death usually causes too much scratching. Scratching leads to disease, and trust me, when they develop a vaccine, the human surviving 1% people will get it first, then the healthy zombies. That puts you outside the 'alpha zombie zone'. Either trap the dogs and cats in cupboards, or let them loose outside, let them be someone else's problem. Let the humans waste their ammunition on pets, not you!

OTHER FOOD SOURCES

Butcher shops hold meat. Supermarkets will have passable meat for a while. And don't think that only human food will suffice. Dog food, cat food, fish food all will supply enough nutrients to hopefully last you through to the vaccine stage.

I know you want human food, but take a look around you.... Right now. What else do you see that would could curb your craving just a little bit?

To survive as a zombie until help/vaccine arrives, you have to think outside the box.

Just because you crave a bit of next door's leg, doesn't mean you have to give into your cravings.

GUN/HUNTING STORES

Humans will try to arm themselves, so in the initial days after the Zombie Holocaust/Apocalypse, gun shops and hunting stores will be a source of fresh meat, freshly killed human surviving 1% meat, lying on the streets outside the shops. (Probably with gunshot wounds and arrows sticking in them)

Try to eat in the evening, you're a much harder target then, and no matter how bad the apocalypse is, humans cannot rid themselves of the habit of sleeping at night.

TIP; if you see bright red dots on you or your immediate associates, shuffle away as fast as you can. The red dot means they're using infra-red sights on their guns or crossbows. They are deadly accurate with those, even the silly frail humans that can't shoot normal guns.

SHOPPING MALLS

For some reason, in times of Zombie Apocalypse, humans gravitate to shopping malls. They think they're safe, there's multi levels, and usually a food superstore. This is why you have a hammer.

(Admit it, you have wondered about the hammer all along, haven't you?)

One even unwieldy tap on tempered glass will shatter it. Humans inside a mall are like lobsters in a pool.

Even an uncoordinated zombie can break into a shopping mall in minutes. This is why you have a hammer on your hip.

Watch their human smug faces turn to mortal fear as you slowly push to the front of the zombies pressing on the mall's glass doors and start to tap on the windows with your hammers.

There is also an inherent safety in large zombie numbers. Gather friends and family, and go looking for food together.

This is a great tactic, it panics the heck out of already scared humans, and let's face it, unless they have unlimited ammunition, they can't realistically shoot you all. The laws of statistics favor the 99% crowd.

SHINY METAL BOXES

"Packed like lemmings into shiny metal boxes…" Sting's lyric in the Police song; Synchronicity 2 couldn't describe the human race to find loved ones better. These shiny metal boxes are fantastic when they've got petrol/gas and the room on the roads to move. But when they're in traffic jams, they're like cans of sardines. Food packed, just ready for you to open the container. And remember, car glass is toughened, and easily tapped/shattered by the slightest of hammer blows.

Also when the shiny metal boxes run out of fuel, humans become focused on getting gas/petrol for their vehicles. It makes them do silly things, even leaving their smaller food human groups in the car while they go looking for gas. Sardine cans.

MOANING

Short point; learn to stop moaning. Be a silent zombie. Be the top of your species; the alpha-zombie. The ninja zombie.

ZOMBIE STEP 11

FINDING SAFETY

Okay; in case of Zombie Holocaust/Apocalypse, being safe is all about two things. Not being dead (and here I'm talking about being absolutely dead, not the zombie 'un-dead' crap), and not dying.

Technically, the best way to survive the Zombie Holocaust/Apocalypse is to put a sign on your door saying;

"Zombie locked in the basement, please come in when the vaccine is developed!"

Then go downstairs and lock yourself in the basement and wait.

But it would make a boring movie, and probably has some other issues along the way that I've not considered. You'd probably gnaw your legs off or something. Not a pretty sight for the arriving paramedics.

ZOMBIE STEP 12

ZOMBIE SEX GUIDE

Be careful.

Be very careful.

And in case you didn't get the idea without me giving away too much information…

Zombie appendages are fragile, they can rip off or fall off at a moment's notice. If it went wrong, an orgy at a zombie's house could look like a cloakroom at a leper's convention.

But zombie sex is not all bad, if things got, shall we say; "Carried away." Perhaps you could eat the things that you carry away!

Overshare?

I'm sure by now I've lost most of my readers, so I'm as well stopping.

The humans have gotten bored, and the zombies have all wandered off… hopefully with their Zombie Bibles in their back pockets.

Here's the additional guides I promised you;

(A lot of investigative journalism has gone into these guides, and I hope you appreciate the hours of research involved.)

Children's Zombie Survival Guide

Same as above except;

Make sure your father/mother zombie puts a sign on your chest. It MUST be the sign you've been forced to carry everywhere for years.

If there's no sign; shuffle like the wind; you're the next meal. Avoid rabid pets. Gravitate to Grandma's house; she's less likely to eat you, and probably slower than you anyway.

(This is the secret reason grandparents and grandkids get on so well. They KNOW they're going to be partnered up against the parents in times of Zombie Holocaust/Apocalypse.)

Pets Zombie Survival Guide

Get out of the house. Gravitate to the hills, eat the shuffling children and the other shuffling pets.

Grandparent's Zombie Survival Guide

Same as above except;

You are food. Distrust everyone except grandkids. Kill all pets now while you've got the chance.

Pregnant Mother's Zombie Survival Guide

Same as above, but one more job with the black Sharpie.

Write high on thighs;

"Small creature coming out soon. Do Not Eat."

Second job with black Sharpie. Write on arms; "Write this on baby's forehead; "I am your baby, do not eat me.""

When baby is four years old, tape the child sign to his/her chest and let him/her run to grandma's house.

Liberal's Zombie Survival Guide

Same as above except;

Before the Zombie Holocaust/Apocalypse you never believed in the second amendment, you were against guns.

If you're now a zombie, well done, you were actually on the right side.

If you're a human survivor, yeah, I know; you changed your mind pretty bloody quick, didn't you.

Conservative's Zombie Survival Guide

Same as above except;

Before the Zombie Holocaust/Apocalypse you wanted lots of guns.

If you are a zombie, you are one sorry chappie.

If you're a human survivor, go for it Rambo, you got it right, but watch out for the zombie hammers.

THE END.

This guide will be updated with relevant information.

If you think you have information which would be an advantage to zombie survival, please email me;

hallandmillar@gmail.com

I will sift through the detritus and consider anything remotely comical/satirical/sarcastic.

Look out for more releases at;

www.ianhallauthor.com

8786549R00045

Printed in Great Britain
by Amazon.co.uk, Ltd.,
Marston Gate.